A. A. Livingston • Illustrated by Joey Chou

B. Bear and Lolly
Catch That Cookie!

SCHOLASTIC INC.

For my dad, with love.
—A.A.L.

*To my mother, and to all
the mama bears in the world.*
—J.C.

ISBN 978-1-338-26680-1
Copyright © 2015 by HarperCollins Publishers. All rights reserved. Published by Scholastic Inc., 557 Broadway, New York, NY 10012, by arrangement with HarperCollins Children's Books, a division of HarperCollins Publishers. SCHOLASTIC and associated logos are trademarks and/or registered trademarks of Scholastic Inc.

12 11 10 9 8 7 6 5 4 3 2 1   18 19 20 21 22 23

Printed in the U.S.A.   08

This edition first printing, January 2018

The artist used Adobe Illustrator to create the digital illustrations for this book.
Typography by Martha Rago

B.Bear and Lolly were the best of friends.
And why not? They liked the same porridge, the same
chair, and the same comfy bed.

One day, B. Bear and Lolly were hard at work on a new invention: the Porridge Perfecter.

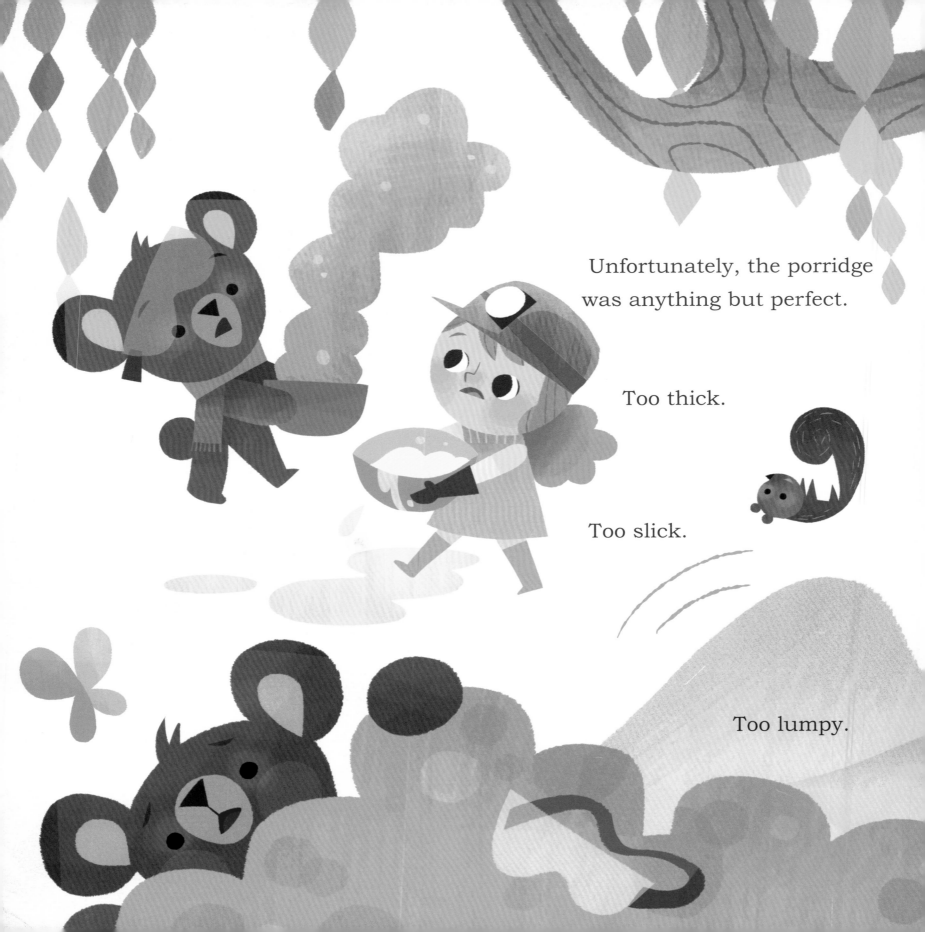

Unfortunately, the porridge was anything but perfect.

Too thick.

Too slick.

Too lumpy.

. . . the Gingerbread Man burst into the clearing and ran right through their invention.

BAM!

The Porridge Perfecter teetered . . .

it tottered . . .

and it toppled over!

B. Bear tried not to cry. "The Gingerbread
Man didn't even say he was sorry. He just
ran off."

Lolly wasn't sad—she was mad.
"*And* he didn't stay to help clean
up his mess! Let's go get him!"

The chase was on!

But they just couldn't catch
that cookie.

The Gingerbread Man looked back and sang:
"*Run, run, as fast as you can.*
You can't catch me—
I'm the Gingerbread Man!"

"Ooh!" shouted Lolly.
"I just want to crumble
that cookie!"

B. Bear had a plan. He made a map, rigged a net, and was ready to snatch his catch! When the Gingerbread Man zoomed by, B. Bear pulled the rope . . .

. . . and missed.

Lolly giggled. "Close,
but no cookie!"

It was time for Lolly's plan. She made a scary mask to stop the Gingerbread Man in his tracks.

When the Gingerbread Man ran by, she jumped out and yelled,

"BOO!"

But the Gingerbread Man was *so* scared, he ran away even faster than before!

"Oh, golly, Lolly!" said B. Bear. "We'll never catch the Gingerbread Man. He's just too fast!"

Back at the clearing, B. Bear's stomach gurgled and growled.

"Porridge! That's it!" he said.

The two friends set a perfect porridge
trap. When the Gingerbread Man rounded
a corner,

he slipped . . .

he slid . . .

and he was stuck!

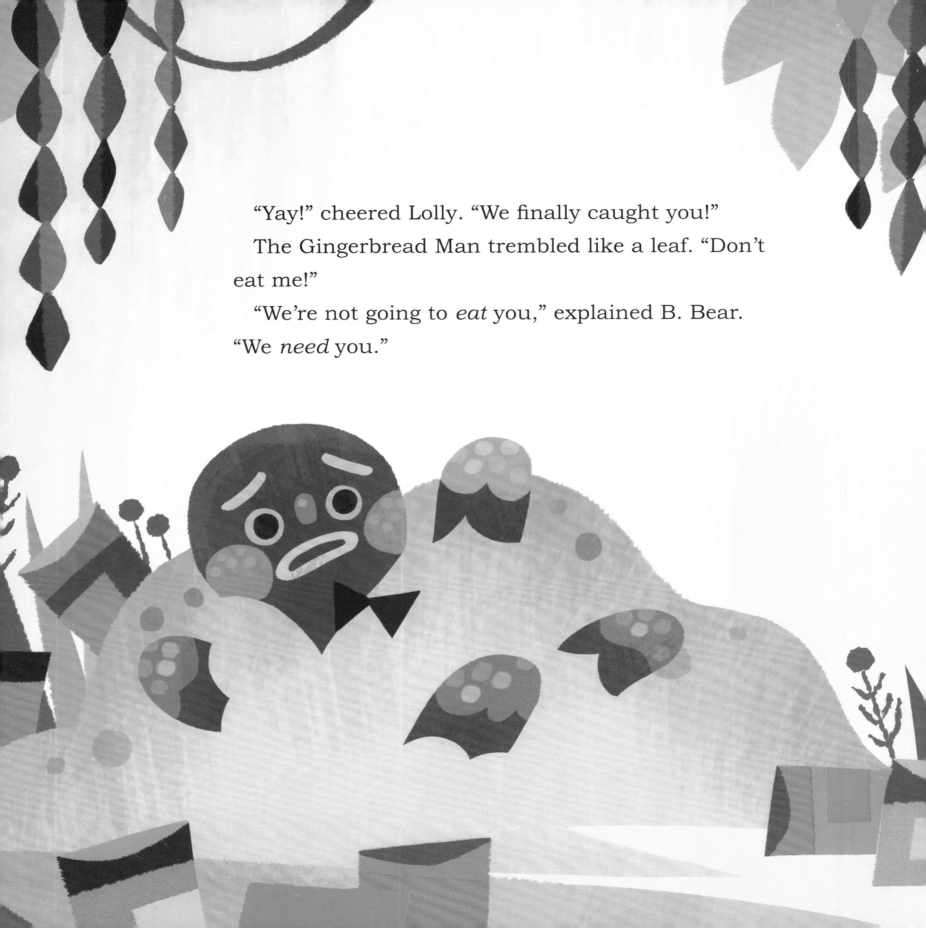

"Yay!" cheered Lolly. "We finally caught you!"

The Gingerbread Man trembled like a leaf. "Don't eat me!"

"We're not going to *eat* you," explained B. Bear. "We *need* you."

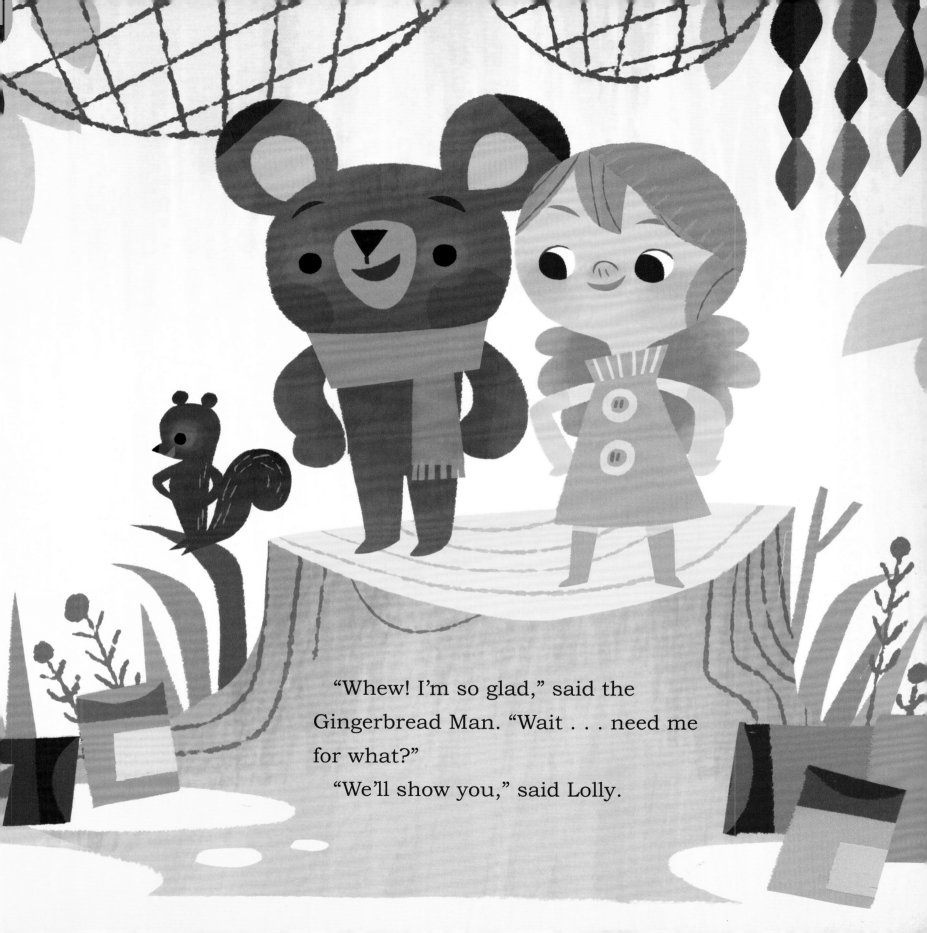

"Whew! I'm so glad," said the
Gingerbread Man. "Wait . . . need me
for what?"
"We'll show you," said Lolly.

"Goodness gumdrops!" said the Gingerbread Man when he saw the giant mess. "I'm so sorry! How about if I help you put it back together?"

"That's *exactly* what we were thinking," said Lolly.

When they were done rebuilding the
Porridge Perfecter, the machine looked great.
"There's only one problem," said B. Bear.
"We *still* can't make perfect porridge."

The Gingerbread Man offered to help. "It's the least I can do."

He checked the water. He checked the oats.

"Aha!" he said finally. "There's no spoon! You need to keep the porridge moving—just like me!"

So he spun it . . .

he swirled it . . .

and he stirred it up.

He even thought of a new song:

"*Stir, stir, as fast as I can.*
Who's making porridge?
The Gingerbread Man!"

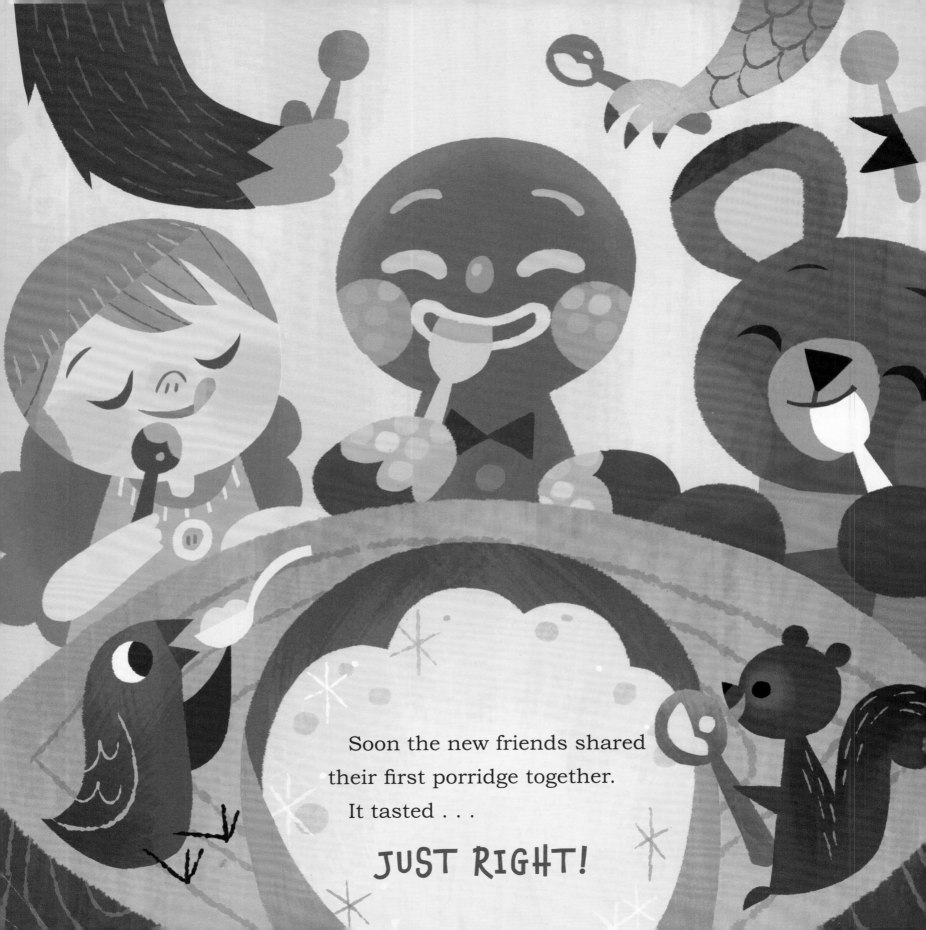

Soon the new friends shared
their first porridge together.
It tasted . . .

JUST RIGHT!